Beneath the Bed
and Other Scary Stories

Mister Shivers

Beneath the Bed

and Other Scary Stories

WRITTEN BY
MAX BRALLIER

ILLUSTRATED BY
LETIZIA RUBEGNI

ᐁACORN™
SCHOLASTIC INC.

For my Dad. My favorite sounding board,
my favorite writer, my favorite guy. —MB

To Cri, Agata, and Tancredi, for teaching me how to turn
scary monsters into funny creatures. —LR

Text copyright © 2019 by Max Brallier
Illustrations copyright © 2019 by Letizia Rubegni

Library of Congress Cataloging-in-Publication Data

Names: Brallier, Max, author. | Rubegni, Letizia, illustrator.
Title: Beneath the Bed and Other Scary Stories / written by Max Brallier ;
illustrated by Letizia Rubegni.
Description: First edition. | New York, NY : Acorn/Scholastic Inc., 2019. |
Series: Mister Shivers ; 1 | Audience: Ages 5–7. | Summary: The kids at
school dare John to visit the old house on the hill at night, and when he
and his sister go in they find dusty dishes set on the table, a book open
like it is waiting for a reader, and something hiding under the bed in the
attic—and that is only one of the five scary stories with unexpected
twists that are included in this collection.
Identifiers: LCCN 2018047608 | ISBN 9781338318531 (pbk. : alk. paper) |
ISBN 9781338318548 (hardcover : alk. paper)
Subjects: LCSH: Fear—Juvenile fiction. | Horror tales. | Children's stories,
American. | CYAC: Horror stories. | Short stories. | LCGFT: Horror fiction.
Classification: LCC PZ7.B7356 Be 2019 | DDC 813.6 [Fic] —dc23 LC record available at
https://lccn.loc.gov/2018047608

10 9 8 7 6 5 4 3 2 1   19 20 21 22 23

Printed in China   62
First edition, September 2019
Edited by Katie Carella
Book design by Maria Mercado

TABLE OF CONTENTS

Dear Reader,

I like stories that are cold, dark, and surprising — just like the stories in this book.

A strange box was left on my doorstep. A dead mouse sat beside it. Here is what I found inside:

- A tree branch.
- A doll's eye.
- A piece of an old quilt.
- A toy's rusty head.

There was also a notebook in the box. This note was taped to it:

PROMISE ME, MR. SHIVERS, THAT YOU WILL SHARE THE STORIES INSIDE THIS BOOK.

So, this book is my promise. I pass these stories to you, and I hope you like scary stories. Because these stories will make you shiver.

Mister Shivers

BENEATH THE BED

Kids at school said the old house on the hill was full of **ghosts**.

The kids dared me to visit the house.
They dared me to visit **at night**.
They dared me to visit **every** room.

I begged my sister Beth to go with me.
After I asked five times, she said,
"Okay."

Beth and I walked up to the house.
The wind howled.

Beth said, "John, I am scared."

"Me too," I said. "But if we don't do this, the kids at school will say we're scaredy-cats."

We walked up the porch steps.

The wood moaned,
like it was warning us to stop.

The house felt alive.

I pushed open the door.
We took deep breaths.

"Come on," I said
as we stepped inside.

In the kitchen, dusty dishes sat
on the table.

In the living room, a sofa was covered
with a sheet.

In the library, a book sat open
like it was waiting for a reader.

There was only one room left to visit:
the attic bedroom.

Beth and I went
up,
up,
up.

The bedroom was cold and damp.
And **dark**.

I gasped.

Two tiny lights glowed beneath
the bed.

Beth grabbed my hand.
"Those lights look like eyes,"
she whispered.

A chain hung from the ceiling.
My hand shook as I tugged it.

CLICK! Light filled the room.

A doll sat beneath the bed.

Beth giggled. "They **are** eyes,"
she said. "They are only the small,
painted eyes on an old doll."

"There are no ghosts in this house!"
I said, smiling.

"That is right," the doll said.
"It is just the three of us."

A HAIR DOWN TO MY STOMACH

When I woke up, my throat was scratchy.

There was a **hair** in my throat!
It felt like it went all the way down
to my stomach.

I ran to my mother's room. "Mother!"
I said. "There is a hair in my throat!"

My mother looked inside my mouth.
"I see it," she said. "There is a hair
all the way down to your stomach!"

My mother tried to pull the hair out,
but she was not able.

She told me not to worry.

She said it would go away.

But it did not
go away.

Days went by.

My throat was
very scratchy.

I felt sick in
my belly.

My mother took me to the doctor.

I opened wide and said, "AHH!"

The doctor said, "I see the problem.
There is a hair all the way down
to your stomach."

She reached into my mouth.
She felt around.

"I have the hair!" the doctor said
at last.

She pulled and pulled.
But what she pulled out
was not a hair.

It was…

A mouse!

"You should not sleep with your
mouth open," the doctor said.
"This mouse crawled all the way
down to your stomach!"

THE STATUE

I was at a yard sale
with my mom.
She was looking at
a creepy statue
of a man.

The statue
stood as big
as a real man.
The man's lips
were pressed tight
together in a frown,
like he was cold.

A tattered quilt was wrapped
around the statue.

The quilt was full of holes.

I didn't like the quilt.
It smelled old.

"Never take the quilt off the statue," a voice said in my ear.

I jumped. The lady who ran the yard sale stood behind me. She was dressed like a witch.

My skin prickled.
An icy breeze swept across the yard.
Suddenly, I felt **very cold**.

"Mom," I said. "Don't buy that statue!"

But my mom bought the statue.
The lady threw in the quilt for free.

At home, my mom placed the statue
in our living room.

The statue—and the quilt—gave me
the creeps.

I ran up to my room to get away
from them.

But I could not stop thinking about
the smelly quilt. I could smell it
all the way upstairs.

Later that night, I tiptoed downstairs.

I marched up to the statue—and
yanked off the quilt!

I ran outside and threw it in the trash.

Then I went back to bed.
I pulled my warm blanket
up to my chin.

I wasn't asleep for long.

I woke up cold.
My teeth were chattering.
I looked around.

My blanket was **gone**!

The yard sale lady's warning
raced through my head:
"Never take the quilt off the statue."

I rushed downstairs.

My warm blanket was wrapped
around the statue! And now the statue
was smiling.

A DARK AND STORMY NIGHT

Oliver always left his toys outside.

On Saturday, Oliver's dad said,
"Bring in your toys before bed."

Oliver said, "I will, Dad."

But Oliver forgot.

It rained and Mighty Joe got wet.

Now Mighty Joe was rusty.

On Sunday, Oliver's mom said,
"Bring in your toys before bed."

Oliver said, "I will, Mom."

But Oliver forgot.

A cat came into the yard and chewed
on Buddy Bear.

Now Buddy was a one-eyed bear.

On Monday, Oliver was sound asleep when—

KRAK! The sound of thunder woke him up.

Rain pounded against his window. Lightning lit up his room.

Oliver's heart raced. "Oh no!" he said. "I left my toys outside again!"

Oliver rushed to his window.
He looked outside.

But his toys were not there!

Just then, his bedroom door creaked open.

Oliver's toys stood in his doorway! They looked **wet** and **angry**.

Buddy's one eye glared at him.

Oliver scrambled back on his bed.
"I'm sorry!" he cried.

"It's too late for that!" Mighty Joe
yelled. "You left us out in the rain
for the last time!"

The toys slowly marched
toward Oliver.

Then the bedroom door slammed shut.

THE NOISE AT THE WINDOW

My family moved to an old red house.
The house sat in the middle of a field.
It looked lonely.

My new bedroom smelled like
dust and cobwebs.

Our first night in the house,
my mother and father tucked me in.
"Sweet dreams, Lucy," they said.

I pulled the blankets **close** and
shut my eyes **tight**.
Then I heard a noise.

SCRAAAPE!
SCRAAAAAAAPE!

"AHHHH!" I yelled.

The noise stopped.

My father rushed into my room.

"Somebody was clawing at
my window!" I told him.

"Lucy," he said with a sigh.
"You only heard branches scraping
against the glass."

"Oh. Okay," I said.

I pulled my blankets **closer**.

I shut my eyes **tighter**.

I began to drift to sleep when—

SCRAAAPE

SCRAAAAAAAPE!

"AHHHH!" I yelled.

51

The noise stopped.

My mother flung open the door.

"Somebody was clawing at
my window!" I told her.

"Lucy," she said with a sigh.
"You only heard branches scraping
against the glass."

"Okay," I said softly.

I pulled my blankets **even closer**.
I shut my eyes **even tighter**.

Finally, I fell asleep.

In the morning, my bedroom was
bright and sunny.

I heard birds chirping outside.

I remembered the tree that had scared
me the night before.

I rushed to my window.

Then I froze.

There was no tree outside my window.
There were no trees near the house
at all.

But there were **scratches** across
the window. And I could feel them
on the inside of the glass.

ABOUT THE CREATORS

MAX BRALLIER is the *New York Times* and *USA Today* bestselling author of more than thirty books including The Last Kids on Earth series, the Eerie Elementary series, and the Galactic Hot Dogs series. Max lives in New York with his wife and daughter.

LETIZIA RUBEGNI is a children's book illustrator. At an early age, she fell in love with storytelling through pictures. She carries her red sketch pad everywhere she goes to capture any interesting ideas. She lives in Tuscany, Italy.

1. Draw the head and ears.

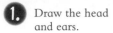

2. Draw the body, plus two arms and two legs.

3. Draw an oval-like shape on the face and on the belly.

4. Draw one eye and one eye socket. Add details to the ears.

5. Draw a vertical line on the face and on the belly. Add a nose.

6. Color in your drawing!

WHAT'S YOUR STORY?

Oliver's toys are mad at him for leaving them outside.
The story in this book ends when the door slams.
Imagine what happens next.
What do **you** think the toys say to Oliver?
Write and draw a scary story!